SOX
UNPLUGGED

SOX
UNPLUGGED

The Story Coloring Book

Chris Gillam
Illustrations by Shelley Abrahamse

authorHOUSE®

AuthorHouse™ UK Ltd.
1663 Liberty Drive
Bloomington, IN 47403 USA
www.authorhouse.co.uk
Phone: 0800.197.4150

The cover and all interior illustrations are illustrated by Shelley Abrahamse

Published by AuthorHouse   08/29/2014

ISBN: 978-1-4969-9024-2 (sc)
ISBN: 978-1-4969-9023-5 (e)

Any people depicted in stock imagery provided by Thinkstock are models, and such images are being used for illustrative purposes only.
Certain stock imagery © Thinkstock.

This book is printed on acid-free paper.

Contents

Chapter 1

It was a normal day like any other, I have a routine much like any cat on the block, wake up, stretch out and head for the kitchen, after breakfast bounce out the window and visit all my mates who have done pretty much the same thing in the last hour.

We all met on the paving of the complex to discuss the events of the night, which chased which rat around, which had a fight and just general banter. We lived in a townhouse complex of eight units, I lived in unit number eight, the pool and entertainment area was directly across from my unit, my best cat buddy Rufus lived in the unit number six, next to the pool. Rufus was my protector, he was much older than me and there were many cats in the complex, none that I really knew and all rather aggressive. I was the youngest in the complex.

I am rather a nerd, not a fighting man. Quiet the coward actually. Rufus protected me from the general conflict and territory fighting of the complex. My good man Rufus belonged to an old woman, who was kindly, lived alone and seldom had any visitors. Most cats in the complex had their own humans but there were a few visitors who just liked beating some of us up for the fun of it. Rufus always watched out for trouble makers, he prided himself on being able to spot trouble.

My human people were a man, a woman and a child, my first memories of them were feet, little feet of the little boy, he must have been hiding me as I seemed to live under a bed for an awful long time but as I got older the woman took care of my food and I did not see much of the dad of the house. The mom yelled a lot especially when she saw me oddly enough. I was not allowed to scratch the furniture, sit on the tables, I mean really? How was I supposed to be if I could not be me? I did not know why my nails just wanted to rip the furniture, they just went to it and I followed them.

I should have known something was different about this week, I had seen boxes being packed up and standing around in my house over the past few days, I did not think much of it as there always seemed to be boxes of goods being brought in and taken out of the house and certainly nothing to worry about, my owners always had family or friends staying over for short periods so there was a lot of movement of goods and luggage. Humans had very different ways of doing things to cats but my life was puurfect! Food, lots of stroking and affection, compliments and a warm spot to sleep at night.

Was my life about to change or what?

It was evening and getting dark, being summer that was rather late. I had had a good day out, lying around, grooming myself, showing off, I liked showing off, the girls liked me a lot and always smiled and winked at me. Rufus told me I was too young for that kind of attention but I knew I had nice teeth, green eyes, sleek grey body, long whiskers and two white socks.

I climbed through the security gate and headed up to the door, looked up to my usual window to jump in and it was closed, with no way in from this side of the house so I walked back through the security gate of the garage and around the complex to the front of my house and came through the garden gate, the house was closed up too, no windows open, I climbed onto the window sill to look inside, blackness looked back, not a light in the place, but worse, not a stick of furniture either. I went to all the windows I could get to and peeped in, reaffirming my horror. I felt my blood draining to my four feet, my heart beating like a drum in my ears, I felt my face become hot under my fur, I was sweating, this was panic. Where was my stuff, where were my peoples stuff, our stuff, my people?

They had left, my people had gone, without me? Abandoned me? What was I to do?

I felt weak, sick, my eye sight seemed fuzzy. My head felt hot. I ran over to my buddy, I felt dizzy and not quiet orientated. I could not believe my eyes; this could not be happening I kept telling myself.

Rufus was about to settle in for his dinner, waiting around the ankles of his owner, rubbing himself on her legs, doing the usual thing we cats do to show our appreciation of our dinner. I jumped up on his kitchen window sill and called out to him, "Buddy, Rufus, you gotta see this..."

Rufus looked at me in surprise, it was not normal for anyone to disturb his dinner; this was his special time with his human. He looked longingly at his bowl of what appeared to be delicious meat and gravy with bits of carrots and beans and back at me trying to decide which one to attend to first. He gave me the benefit of the doubt and jumped up onto the window.

"What is it now?" he said irritably.

"Rufus, they have gone, they left me" I could feel the tears coming in both panic and fear.

"Did you drink the bad water again? No, Buddy, you have to be mistaken, let me come over with you and have a look".

I ran ahead, he was older and slower, I wished he would hurry up and run with me. We went to the front of the house and peered through the windows together. For good measure he jumped up onto the side wall and crossed over the patio roof and looked into the bedroom window, he looked sick too, his eyes wider than usual, "they have indeed gone Buddy" he said. "They must have done what humans call a runner. That is when they do not pay the rent, they vanish like this. I have seen it time and again…"

"Well that is educational Rufus, but how does it help me?, I am so afraid, what will I do? They left me."

He looked worried, that was not reassuring at all.

"Nothing can be solved on an empty stomach, my boy, let's go and share my dinner and we will think of something after." he said.

I did not have much of an appetite right now, but clearly Rufus's mind was more on his dinner than on my problems. We went back to his house and his human was in the lounge watching TV again, her main pastime. Rufus ate the major portion of his supper and left me a bit, after I ate I wished he had left me more, it was very good indeed.

We went back out of the unit and sat on the pool wall. The wind had picked up and the rain was clearly going to break shortly. My house was all locked up, where was I going to sleep during the rain

I wondered. As if reading my mind Rufus said, "the rain is coming, you'd better come home with me, you can hide until my human goes to bed and you will have to leave early before she wakes up".

It was a plan, I was actually afraid to sleep outside; I had never slept outside before. Cats do get scared too.

I was comfortable enough in Rufus's house, but it was not mine. Rufus tended to show off a little, the big TV, the antique furniture he scratched on, the fluffy rug he slept on, he made me feel worse than I was already feeling. The place did have an odd smell about it though, old and musty but I was grateful nonetheless. I thanked him for his hospitality and left early before breakfast. A mistake I discovered later on in the day when my stomach growled with hunger. I had not completely realised the direness of my situation until now.

I lay on the wall watching the main gate optimistically, each time a car entered I sat up, hoping for my humans to return, a sign of them, the car, the yelling mother, the annoying kid with the ball, I would take anything right now but as the day wore on and my hunger grew I knew they were not coming back and I realised I was homeless. My mind screamed "homeless" at me. Homeless. Homeless.....

I went back to my house many times during the day, I went to check, maybe they would be back, maybe this was all just a bad dream, maybe the furniture would be back but it remained closed up and empty.

Rufus came by now and then, sitting for a while on the wall with me, watching the cars in and out the complex, rattling off about the neighbours until dinner time when his human called him in for his dinner.

He invited me to join him but seemed less enthusiastic. I think he did it more out of politeness than anything else. He ate first and left me as little as the night before. I was seriously hungry and the taste of his dinner made me hungrier. I slept behind his humans couch again. Listening to any car sound, I checked under the curtain, nothing. I listened to my hungry noisy stomach. I was depressed, knowing that I could not live permanently like this with a tit bit of dinner and in another home where I clearly did not belong.

I fell into a sleep of wonderful dreams of my humans being back to waken to a shrill voice screaming at me to get out. Rufus's human had woken early and seen me in the house. I skedaddled out of the place into the pouring rain. Instinctively and out of habit I ran to my house through the security gate and sat in the garage, it was cold, the floor bare cement with a large oil stain, oh I loved that oil stain, my humans car made that stain. There was nothing warm to lie on, nothing to form a barrier between me and the floor. Oh my word! What was I to do? I realised my butt was quiet a skinny one, not much to sit on.

I looked around the garage, four bare walls and an empty shelf with nothing on it but dust and too high for me to jump onto and a hook where the ugly grass hat once hung. My humans garden hat, now also gone. Oh my word. Oh my word.

My bedroom, my little buddy and my soft things were all gone.

Chapter 2

I was now on my own, I was terrified. Every noise made me jump. I had a bare garage, a concrete floor and an oil stain for company.

I no longer had dinner with Rufus, his human watched out for me and for a strange reason took a dislike to me, screaming at me or throwing things at me. I decided she was not such a nice human after all, she was mean spirited.

I spent a lot of time lying in front of my empty house, the other cats both domestic and wild visited me and seemed more friendly than before.

One scabby mix brown, black and white coloured wild cat took pity on me and introduced me to the wonderful world of garbage.

I was lying against the wall of my house in the sun thinking about my people and he marched over to me, I felt my heart beat fast in my chest, he was a known fighter. I expected the worst.

"Are you hungry" he said as he was just about on top of me.

My eyes went big, my mouth dried and I squeaked out a "yes".

"Well then boy, come and eat, there is plenty, it is Friday" and he began to walk off. He looked back and I jumped to follow him. I had visions of meat and gravy in mind.

We went out of the complex by jumping into the tree and over the wall, to the garbage on the pavement, the many black bags which the truck came to collect each week. This was as far from my visions as could be.

He had lived on garbage for a long time and was accustomed to the filthy smell and rotten bits of old and discarded food to be found in the garbage bags which lay feted and sweating out in the sun waiting for the refuse removal to collect them.

The terrible smell of the bin liners, the sweat of garbage was too much for me. My empty stomach lurched into my mouth, I pretended to cough, I tried sharing his enthusiasm, I tried to convince myself it was not so bad, it was just food thrown out, wasted, unwanted. The reality was too awful, I was grateful to find a chicken bone; I chewed on it a little. A very little. It was sour with rot. I tried another bag, I found some old bread, grey with mould and I found some brown stuff, unidentifiable but ate it. The wild cats tucked in.

When the truck came we all ran back over the wall into the complex but the wild cats showed me where the garbage is generally stored around the back of the units and told me that anytime I wanted to I could join them, best times to come was mornings.

I tried to fill my hungry stomach with the putrid mess in the bags every day but I grew ill with cramps and throwing up. Fresh water was also difficult so I had two choices, rain water in the ditches or puddles or pool water with chlorine in it. Neither were pleasant options. The puddles always had a film of dust on them or were muddy and the pool water tasted bad.

Life was unbearable, it had been weeks since my people left me, I was thin and gangly, I could feel my hip bones protruding when I sat down, my arms were scrawny, my head looked too big for my skinny body and my ears looked more like boat sails than ears. I had gone from a growing cat to something I did not recognise in the reflection of the windows I went to check into each day in hope of seeing my people again. In my heart I knew they were not coming back, but I could not stop myself checking anyway. I was drawn to the place, my old home, my home. The only home I had known.

I slept in the sun in front of my house, too afraid to go far off in case my people came back. What if... and I was not there? I could not bear the thought. I was so torn. In a small way just being close to the house gave me some comfort. I wanted to believe they would come back, come looking for me and fetch me to our new home, our new home with soft things and food smells and bowls of milk. I was losing my mind in dreams; my favourite thing to do now was sleep and dream of being home and having people again.

I was embarrassed and shamed to share my thoughts with Rufus, he seemed to get irritated with me a great deal, even avoided me at times, especially around meal times.

A car pulled up. I was excited, I jumped up to see who arrived. A lady got out of the grey car. She was going to my house. A human at my house. My heart beat faster in my chest. I ran up next to her, greeted her, rubbed against her legs. She had keys, keys to my house. She unlocked the security gate I could so easily walk through to sit in the garage and she unlocked the wooden door and opened the door. I ran in ahead of her.

Oh wonders, my house, the smell of it, I was in. She was looking into each room. I ran next to her legs up the stairs to show her each room was empty, I was telling her about my situation, I explained I was left alone, I asked about my people, I ran down the stairs again with her. She opened up the cupboards, I ran into them, she shooed me out. I told her who lived in each room, what was in each cupboard but she seemed pre-occupied, disinterested in me, maybe she did not speak cataneeze.

She walked out, I went with her, she locked up and got back into the car, she left.

I was alone again but happy I had been back in my house, the smells of it, oh how I missed my people. Who was this woman, how did she get our keys? So much to think about but the joy of being inside my house kept my heart warm for now.

I ran over to tell Rufus all about my house and the visitor, that I was inside the house, that it was totally empty, that I had seen inside the cupboards and all the toys and books were gone, all the old shoes I had slept in and the bed I slept under, all gone. I told him about the woman, she put lights on and off, she ran the taps, she made notes on a book.

He was excited enough to share his dinner with me. He wanted me to tell him every detail. I did. Real food again, I did not want to show Rufus just how desperate I was, I had some pride left but I enjoyed his dinner so much that I could not resist licking the bowl and my whiskers for the last bits but I immediately went back to my house after dinner in case she came back. I slept on the cold concrete again watching the rain trickle at the bottom of the gates, jumping up at any sign of car lights. I just knew she was going to come, someone was going to come. At every sound of a car I was up, looking, listening, my heart banging in my chest with anticipation. Sleep did not come easily.

The people that lived in the unit next to my house used their garage as a storage unit and parked their car in the carport, the garage seemed ever growing in items from garden refuse to boxes of unwanted books, this attracted the attention of rats, nasty, fat rats who were always scuttling around during the night, running from bush to garage, from waste bins back to their hiding places in the mess of storage. In my misery and loneliness I did not notice them running past me at night until I heard a small voice this particular night.

"Hey you, everything okay?" I looked around trying to find the voice to find it peeping at me from under the gate, small black ever moving eyes, and whiskers twitching, long nose moving constantly, long ugly yellow teeth.

I sat straight up.

"Yes, thank you, I am perfectly alright" I replied, a little shocked that a rat would be talking to me, they are supposed to fear me, I am a cat. Okay admittedly, I was so thin I probably looked like a large relation of his.

"Well-mannered type are you?, must say, you don't look perfectly alright from here, you hungry?"

I stepped closer, food. Was he offering me food? I needed food, after so many days of so little and then eating a little of Rufus's dinner I was now very very hungry.

"I am hungry, why?"

"Oh Okay, then I will just stand out here if you don't mind." he said, and continued with, "saw you had a human here today, she is the owner you know, you are going to get new people staying here, she only comes just before new people come, she rents out the place but they never last here, she is a crook you know, she keeps renting the place out but fixes nothing in it and when the tenants complain she evicts them, a deposit scam I hear."

"Really, is that what happened to my people? She chased them away? how do you know this?"

"Oh, yeah pal, we pretty much know everything, living in the pipes and drains, we hear it all, I've been around, I have. They left in a flash, we knew they were going, they needed to get out before she took their furniture away, yeah, real crook that one. They left you behind did they?"

"Yes, I was out playing and when I came back they were gone.." I could feel the tears in my throat, the sadness overcoming me again. Did they look for me, did they call for me? do they miss me as much as I miss them, oh word, why did I go out that day, my mind raced.

The little beady eyes looked deeply into mine "Don't worry pal, you will get new people, if you promise not to eat me or my friends, you can come crash with us, we smell a little off but we are good company and there are some soft boxes next door you can lie on."

I was so starved for company, felt so alone.

"Oh, thank you, I appreciate that so much but I will just wait here for now, thank you for the invitation, I may pop in later" I said. My heart felt like lead in my chest and his kindness made me even more teary.

"Cheers mate" he said as he was leaving.

"Oh, Wait, please wait, what is your name?" He turned back, peering little eyes, twitching little nose.

"Robert, no one gave me that name, I took it, like we rats take most things, the boy who lived here once was Robert, I just like the name, so Robert it is.

What is yours?"

"I don't know, I don't think I have one."

"Okay, I will call you pal for now. Goodnight then", and he was gone, leaving me to think about all he had said, I felt so empty inside, so cold but more confident that I had made a new friend. Robert the rat. So my people did not just run away, they were forced to go. The awful woman made them go. How terrible. I decided I did not like her. Now I worried about them. Were they okay, were they in a house or were they like me in the cold on concrete?

The following day the same car came again, the same woman who could not understand me from the day before, she parked and sat in the car, the "crook". I disliked her, she chased my people. She was waiting for something. Rufus was sitting on the wall waiting, Robert was peeping out of the garage next door from behind a box and more than anyone else, I was waiting. I felt angry.

Another car came, two people got out and walked over to my house. Robert hissed at me to "go in, go in and listen to what they say pal, go" and I did.

There was a tall woman called Su, and a man called Chris. The crook walked up to them, smiling and they did what humans do when they meet, they shook hands.

I ran to them, to the Chris person. He bent down and greeted me with, "hey boy, how you doing" and stroked my head. I replied with, "hi, hello, I am fine, no I am not, I am hungry, are you staying, when are you moving in, I mean, oh, yes, let's go inside..." I could feel myself blushing at falling over my words.

"Well come on then, Let's go look " he said, I could not believe it, he understood cataneeze, he understood me.

The crook unlocked the door and we all went into the house. Su and Chris looked around, Su did most of the talking, Chris was looking at me. He seemed disinterested in the humans. They all went upstairs, I ran with, I was showing them around. The crook was also showing them around, with "and this is the bathroom..." well hello, it has a bath in it what else would it be? and this is the kitchen, again, what would it be if it has a stove in it? I thought.

Chris stroked me again, Oh, I loved it, the human touch, he scratched my ears, oh that was so good. The crook took out some papers, Chris signed the papers and I heard they would move into the house in the next few days. The crook gave Chris a bunch of keys. My keys, our keys to my house. Oh I was thrilled. I preened and rubbed myself on Chris's legs. They all left the house with me next to them all the time. Su looked at me and said, "that must be the neighbours cat".

I shouted "No, I am yours, this is my house." She replied with, "Shame he must be sick, he is so thin." Clearly Su did not speak cataneeze. Chris just stroked me and they left. The two cars drove out of the complex together.

I sat on the bricks waving at them, "Bye" I shouted, "see you soon". No one heard me.

Rufus came over, "looks like you getting new people."

"Oh, yeah" I said, "they moving in this week, they love the place and me" I added lying through my white baby teeth.

"So you'll be moving in then?" he questioned me.

"Oh, definitely" I lied again.

"Well in that case, come over for supper, this is a celebration. You can eat with me every night. When your new people arrive you can share with me for a while." he said with a glint in his eye. It was no secret that Rufus's human had been feeding him the exact same meal for nine years night after night and he was all too keen on a little diversity.

I spotted Robert at the corner of my eye, "Oh, yeah, sure, thanks Rufus, I will be over in a minute, just got to check around the place, just make sure everything is tip top for my people, I will follow you shortly." I said not looking him in the eye.

"Well don't be too long then" and he walked off ahead of me.

I ran over to Robert, "Not technically the truth was that pal?, I think you need some work on your people skills so when your peeps come back you can make your lies true."

"I can't let them think I am homeless any longer, not when people are moving in, I have to make a plan and make these people take me in. Winter is a short way off. I am desperate and Rufus won't share his dinner forever."

"You will charm your way in, I will show you how."

"Not to be rude Robert, but you are a rat who lives in a pipe and garage boxes."

"Trust me, Pal, trust me."

Chris Gillam

Chapter 3

I had dinner with Rufus, he ate the major part of the dinner as always and left me a little with some gravy, I really love gravy and I licked the bowl but I was still so hungry, eating his food made my stomach growl for more. I thanked him and I went to my garage. The concrete was cold even though the day had been warm. Sunlight did into manage its way into the garage. It was still safer for me to sleep inside the garage than to risk being challenged by a larger stray visitor who may be confrontational. I slept with a warmer heart knowing I was not going to be alone here forever.

The day was hot, the sun baking the bricks I was lying on. I had been awake since first light, I was waiting. I watched the main gates of the complex waiting for a sign of the car my people had come in the day before, so fearful they would change their minds and not come. I waited; I changed position a hundred times. I could not settle.

Robert came by, "What's up pal, any signs?"

"Nothing yet, do you think they will still come?"

"Of course, humans move a lot of stuff around, hang in there, they will come." And off he scuttled into the bushes across the complex.

I must have fallen into a deep sleep and was woken by the rattle of the main gates sliding along the track, I jumped up. The big white car again. They were here. "They are here" I shouted to no one in particular, my excitement getting the best of me. The car swung into the parking bay in front of my garage, I ran over to it. Chris greeted me in the same way as he got out the car, a stroke on the head, asked me how I was doing. I answered, "So much better now." he smiled at me. I smiled back.

The passenger got out the car too, she was the cleaning lady. They took buckets and mops from the car. Chris unlocked the house and they went in. The doors were left open. He opened just about every window of the house. I ran through the house, rolled on my back in the still empty lounge, ran to the patio and back into the house. I rolled onto my back in the lounge on the warm tiles where the sun streamed in through the window. Chris came over and stroked my belly and left again saying, "See you later." To the cleaning lady.

"Don't worry about a thing, I will keep an eye on things" I shouted after him.

The house remained open with the cleaning woman in it, I ran in and out of it, checking on the cleaning woman, still not believing that everything was about to change for the better again. Oh I was so happy, my house had people, and my house would have lights and thing in it again. I could have swung through the trees with excitement.

I sat outside on the bricks, caught a glimpse of the other cats looking at me. I pumped up my now tiny chest. My people were coming. I was not homeless anymore. I had status again.

Rufus lay on the wall watching the goings on. Robert popped out of his garage now and then to check on events. My house was the centre of attention now. The human neighbours who walked past looked in and made comments like... "hmm new people again" and "wonder how long that will last", but I was happy. Nothing anyone said today was going to change that. The cleaning woman cleaned every window, every cupboard, every tile and wall and I walked in and out, happy she was there but still worried about my people coming, what was taking so long. I did not show Robert or Rufus my concern, I tried to act casual, tried to relax. The storm was building. I stayed close to my house, I was terrified of thunder and these summer storms cracked the sky with noise and light.

It began raining, at first softly, then really hard, then settled into a fine persistent drizzle. Eventually Chris came back, it was now raining constantly and fairly hard again. I waited in the garage. He was followed by another car with a woman called Sam and two children in it, a little boy named David Erik with glasses and orange hair with freckles on his face and an even smaller girl named Jessica with blond hair.

They off loaded items out of the small car, I ran alongside the boy showing him where to put things, Jessica was being instructed by her mother Sam. They were little people so they could not carry much. Chris off loaded the big white car he drove in. There was a lot of laughing and I laughed to, I don't know why, I was laughing and it felt strange as I had not laughed in so long.

I was so excited, it was real, stuff was coming in. Nice smelling stuff, human stuff. Robert was peeping in from the side gate unnoticed by any human. I ran over to Robert and reported everything. Robert had become my confidant in the last day or so.

"Well old chap, seems like you are going to be fine after all." I don't know why but I wanted to hug him, hug something, I was so happy, my heart was singing with happiness right now. I ran over to the tree and hugged it.

The woman and the children came out of my house and left, Chris and the cleaning lady came out the house next and they locked up the house, the windows were left open, all the windows all around the house, so I jumped up and went through the burglar bars and inside and checked everything.

Very nice things, I smelt everything, very nice smelling things. I rubbed against everything. I lay on the small mats that were put inside the bathrooms; I touched everything at least once. There was no furniture as yet. Robert said furniture came on trucks. I was feeling more at peace. Now that there was stuff in the house and the windows were open, even if they did not come back today, I would still sleep inside tonight on the soft mats in the bathroom, I would not be alone and afraid outside, blocking my ears from the thunder, but it would all be better if they did come today but I would look after things, keep an eye on things as I had promised Chris.

I spent the rest of the day going out and in through the windows, each time another cat came near I jumped up onto the window to show them that this was my house. No strangers thanks.

Habit made me go back outside and watch the gates. The rain had stopped and the sun had come out again. The gates eventually opened and a big truck rambled up the drive, many people jumped out of the back of the truck, the driver of the big truck unlocked the house and carried furniture into the house, so much stuff, I was sure it would never all fit in. I had never seen so much furniture. My old people did not have a quarter of that amount.

I noticed all the floors were now very dirty with the amount of feet and rain water up and down from the truck and into the house and back and forth. The cleaning lady was not going to be pleased about all her hard work being dirtied like this.

Chris and Su were not here yet, I wondered if they know how much stuff was being offloaded, I was beginning to get worried about this, with all this stuff, where we all were going to live, and this was more stuff than what was in Roberts's garage.

Just then the gate rolled open again and there they were, my new people. It was getting late, I could see they were tired but when the doors and boot opened, more stuff, I could not believe it. The inside of the car was packed to the top, the boot was full.

The sky cracked again and the clouds opened up, It poured with rain, hard pelting rain but relentlessly the furniture movers carried in goods, cars came and left, dinner was not forthcoming either and it was already dark so it must have been late as well as it was summer. The truck had now left, the other cars stopped bringing goods and the action had calmed down. I watched all from the corner of the garage. Everything became still and quiet. I told Robert I was going to check on the situation. My stomach was prompting me to check on the situation more than anything else.

I bounced into the house amid the muddy foot tracks already made by humans and my world fell apart again.

I ran headlong into a big ginger tabby cat. "And where do you think you are going young man" his voice boomed at me. I stared, not realising I had in my cowardly fear cringed right up along the doorway trying hard to become one with the doorway itself. My little heart had almost stopped in fright.

"Oh, I am, um, yes, right, I was just..."

"My name is Duke, this is my brother Tangier, he said motioning with his chin at another as big ginger tabby cat, twins I thought, "he is deaf, so he won't hear you and that over there is Tuna", he indicated with a twitch of the ear, "to yet another cat," she is old, really old and really irritable. She has not stopped hissing since I met her some months back, she doesn't like anyone at all", I looked at the dining room table and there sat the blackest cat with the greenest eyes I have ever seen. She was really old and really irritable. This Duke guy was not telling a word of a lie. Immediately she caught my eye she hissed at me.

I looked around the place "uh um, I am still talking young man, and that is my girl, so hands off, her name is Paddles" and he indicated the cutest petite tortoise coloured female peeping at us all through the staircase slats. "and there is no space here for you, so you best move along" Duke continued in his booming voice.

In shock I blurted out, "what do you mean, move along, this is my house, I live here"

"Not anymore it isn't, and we live here now."

Just then the Su human came down the stairs and saw me, "ai, ai, what are you doing here, come on, out you go, home time now" she said and shoed me like I was irritating dust that had blown in.

I bounced out the doorway onto the step. The door slammed shut.

My heart shattered in a million little pieces as I walked away from the door, looking back once to see my dreams vanish like mist in front of the sun.

As I walked to the garage I saw Rufus sitting on the wall watching, He was under the lip of the roof, ensuring the rain did not touch his thick matted coat, I forced myself to look confident and care free as I approached him. "So what's happening?" he asked.

"Oh, no, um, my people are just tired, they are going to get some rest now."

"Hmm, and who are those other cats you were talking to?"

"Um, yeah, well, yes, they are living there too." I said

"And you think with four of them there you are going to live there too?"

"Oh definitely, sure," I lied, "they love me, they are just settling in, sorting a space for me you know how it is."

"No, I don't actually, but as you say, good luck with that pal. I am going to bed, see you tomorrow." He had obviously eaten his dinner already.

I looked after him, wishing I had not let my ego get in the way of truth, I was hungry, I had not eaten since last night. I looked back to my house, the door closed and the lights had gone off, much like my last hope.

"pssst, buddy, hey, chum.... over hear" It was Robert. "that did not go as well as we would have liked huh?, well come along, here, we have some grub. The twit who lives in that place threw out nearly good burgers, a day or three old at most. Kept them in the car and forgot them he did. Let's dig in"

With a half a heart but a full appetite we dug into the bins again.

I lay in the garage under the car next to my oil stain listening to Robert scurrying around with his rat mates, into the pipes, out of the pipes, into the boxes and bushes. I eventually fell asleep, with a heavy heart so wishing I could be inside the house.

The next day the sun shone bright, I had slept the night through dreaming of my life with my new family, who technically did not want me. I took some comfort from the fact that at least I was not totally alone now, there were people living in my house. There were lights on and noises coming from within and talking. I was not alone with the rats and the concrete any longer. They had left garden seat pillows in the garage on the higher shelves and I jumped from the top of the car onto the cushions during the night. It was a wonderful sleep on a lovely soft bed. I was too upset earlier in the evening to notice.

Robert came racing into the garage, sat next to the wheel of the car. "Nice wheels he remarked, slept outdoors again did you?"

"Oh Robert, what am I to do?, they have four cats in there, four!"

"Well here is the thing, it is going to be all about charm."

"Hey?, I mean, sorry, I don't actually know what you are talking about."

"Charm, personality, you have to win them over."

"Really? and how do you suppose I do that?"

"You are going to use that wonderful personality, winning smile and impeccable manners of yours, that's how."

Chapter 4

I watched the door and listened closely for any activity inside. Suddenly the door swung opened and remained open; I could see from the wall I was sitting on that there was a hive of activity inside. I went along the perimeter wall looking into all the windows.

Su was arranging the furniture, Chris was arranging his office, then Su was hanging curtains, it was very busy in there.

More than that I could see the bowl of cat kibble placed right at the front door and my mouth watered. It had been forever since I had had that wonderful taste in my mouth, the explosion of beef and malt flavours on my tongue. I watched as in turn Duke then Tangier, Tuna and the small cat called Paddles nibbled at the bowl. How I envied them all at that moment.

Tuna took up position at the door and hissed generally at everyone. She truly was the most irritable cat I had ever seen. She literally was a body of fur and razor blades.

Everyone seemed to give her space. A lot of it.

Robert and I were in constant consultation over the matter, I was so desperate, I was taking lessons from a rat in how to use my charm, life had taken on a really bleak turn for me as a supposed proud cat to have to take charm lessons from a bin rat but he was my buddy, my only buddy in the whole world. It was no more his fault being born a rat than it was mine to be abandoned.

Rufus had taken on an attitude to me, preferred to ignore me than be my friend now, but I had lied to him by telling him the new people loved me and he did believe that I had a new home.

He may have even have been a little jealous of me now. Reality was I was much in the same place I was in a week ago, homeless. I wish I had not lied to him. I wish I had not lost my buddy. My pride, my ego got the better of me. I had told him of the wonderful things in the house, the soft rugs, the big beds, the lovey couches and I bragged and pretended they were mine. I competed with things that were not mine at all. I was so miserable. I was losing more and more daily. My weight, my hair, my friends and my self-respect. Only Robert knew it was all just fantasy right now.

I was eating out of the bins, but I also had to be stealth about it so that Rufus could not see me doing that. I was so thin I no longer walked, I swaggered like an old time cowboy with too heavy a gun belt. My gun belt being my bony hips. My face had shrunk, my cheek bones stuck out, my eyes huge in my small skull. I was anything but attractive to anyone and certainly not close to cute any longer.

I was lying on the bricks outside the unit for a change of pace when a small sweet voice said, "Hello" I flopped my head back in the direction of the voice. I jumped up immediately seeing it was Paddles. "Hi, I um, Hi" I fumbled out.

"You used to live here, Duke told me all about you." she said.

"Yeah, I mean yes, I do, did, I um..."

"Well, will you show me around then."

I jumped at the chance. She was so sweet and so nice. It had been a while since anyone was that nice to me. I looked past her, no sign of Duke with the big deep voice.

"Sure" I said.

I took her to all the units, showed her all the secret places, I was showing off a little, okay I was showing off a lot. During the hours we spent on the "tour" of the complex I confided in her my sad story of being abandoned. She was just so sweet and nice, I could not help myself.

"That is so sad" she said," some humans are dreadful, I can sneak you in for some food if you want, we have so much we get bored with it. Would you like that?"

Bored with food, how could anyone get bored with food?

"Please, yes, I am so hungry, I would appreciate that very much, and that would be so kind of you."

"Oh, think nothing of it." She smiled.

We spent the afternoon talking. Paddles told me about all the places she had lived in with her people. She told me about her experiences and her friends and the other cats she shared the house with. She said Chris and Su had just gotten married and they all moved together and she liked Duke, he was sweet and said he spoke a lot, Tangier was indeed deaf but he was territorial and a little aggressive, Tuna had lost her people and was adopted by the Chris but she still missed her human mother who had died and that was the reason she was grumpy all the time but at heart she was nice. Paddles said Tuna did not like showing the nice side of herself, but she was quiet sweet in her own way for an old cat. Paddles was

Chris's cat, since she was a baby and she was eight years old now and Duke and Tangier belonged to Su.

She told me she had only known Su for a short time herself but if I wanted to get into the house I needed to charm Chris as he had a very soft heart and was sympathetic to everyone. He always helped everyone and always gave stuff away to people who had little. She told me she did not really know Su but she was strict and yelled far too much for her liking.

Su did not like any of them to sit on the furniture and scratching it was just totally out of the question.

I could not wait for supper time, I was looking so forward to a bite of kibble, I could barely concentrate on my tour of the complex. When we came all the way around again, Robert was hiding under the car against the wheel, watching us. Rufus was sitting on the wall looking hostile. Paddles gave me credibility or rather gave my lie to him credibility. Deep down I was pleased he saw me with Paddles and I shouted over to him that he should come and meet my new friend but he just jumped off the wall towards his own house and ignored me.

"Come around at about sixish, we normally eat then" and she ran into the garage with a wave of her tail.

I ran over to Robert to tell him everything. Every last detail. My throat was dry with talking.

"All very well for you Pal, but she will not tolerate me, she will definitely bite me."

"Why would she do that?"

"I am a rat and she is a cat, which is the way of things. You have been out on your own too long pal!" he said but he looked pleased that I was feeling better.

At six on the nose I was sitting at the open door, the security gate had wide gaps, enough for me to get through, I was so thin, two of me could go through at a time but I did not enter, just sat there not really knowing what to do as an invited guest.

I saw how each cat in the house got issued a bowl of food with gravy, and one big full bowl of milk. Oh it smelled so nice. I felt my mouth watering and had to catch myself from not dribbling on my narrow chest.

All the cats scoffed their food, not giving me a glance, all except Paddles who looked up slightly and winked at me. She took her time, the others had finished when she was only half way. Chris said to her, "no appetite tonight baby girl, moving house is always unsettling" and she looked up and winked at me again through the gate.

Chris said, "okay, I will just leave it here for you for a while." and he left the kitchen.

The other cats had eaten, had a few sips of milk, never went near the kibble bowl and left the kitchen and went to wash their hands and faces with their paws deep within the house.

Paddles was right, they were so over-fed they were bored with their food. I certainly was not over fed or bored.

"Well come on, come and eat if you are going to" she said to me and walked to the door to keep watch. I bolted for the food then remembered my manners, I had to impress her or she may not want to invite me again.

Oh, it was heavenly, the meat and gravy, the soft vegetables, it slid down my throat leaving me looking around for more.

"Drink the milk, there is plenty left over" she said to me.

I did not need a second invitation. It was creamy and warm, oh, it was so good. I gulped it down.

It had been so long since I had tasted milk.

"Go now, quickly, someone is coming." she said

I bolted out the door, shouting back a thank you.

With my tummy full I jumped up onto the bonnet of the car and settled in for the night until Robert popped in.

"Going better is it?" he asked flicking a finger in the air indicating my whiskers, "may want to clean that up hmmm?" Gravy on my whiskers. I licked it off.

I told him about the heavenly meal Paddles shared with me.

I looked at my little friend feeling guilty that I was a cat and he was a mouse.

Paddles would bite him if she could, and yet both of them were my friends.

We chatted about the day, he informed me that Rufus's owner was ill, that the cat in number 3 had had her litter of babies, all five of them, that the refuse had not been removed as there was a utility strike again and that there was to be a mouse and rat meeting later as the cat population had grown in the complex and new rat security and networking had to be discussed. He said he had to leave early for the meeting so I settled down again after turning around a couple of times to find the right position on the car bonnet.

I fell into a deep sleep. I was feeling happier, my belly full of food and milk, I had a new friend and I felt less lonely than I had been in so long.

Chapter 5

With the dawning of a new day I realised that I would have to work really hard to be part of this family and be part of this home, sure I had never lived with so many other cats but I felt I could work around this. I had lived out here for so long, I had fitted into the life of the homeless, I had not been in one fight, strangers had shared their food resources with me and I was generally a nice guy.

The positives so far was that Paddles liked me, we walked around the complex a lot every day, Chris liked me, Tuna did not like anyone so it was not anything personal she had against me, Tangier was deaf and he generally followed his brother Duke's lead, so I had to win over Duke and Su. The odds were not impossible.

Robert said a strategy that rats used was to be as invisible as possible but that I should apply the opposite. Humans feared rats but they liked cats. Humans always said cats were self maintenance animals. Clean and always went to the toilet neatly, cleaning up after themselves. So I should be visible all the time. That way humans would get accustomed to my presence.

I made sure I was visible; I greeted Su in the morning and ensured I was sitting at the door as she was the first to open the front door every morning. Once greeted I walked away; I wanted her to see me but also see I was not going to intrude.

Out of the open door bolted Paddles with her chirpy, "Hi there".

Next came Tangier, he just gave me a glance but with him one never knew for sure, being hearing impaired made him a tad unstable. One minute he just stares at me and the next he is chasing me. Caution with him.

Tuna, well, no explanation there, she seemed to always be in the house, Duke, he was okay with me, just always full of advice to leave his girl alone, problem was she was not leaving me alone. She liked our adventures around the complex, and Duke was also getting old so he did not want to walk all over and climb and jump around but she did and she certainly knew when it was time to go home and eat and never forgot to invite me.

I pretty much lived on the bonnet of the car for some months, eating each night, not well but enough from the left overs of the house cats. Su still believed I was the neighbours cat who just liked hanging around her house. Chris spent more time away from the house than in it, always working. Su worked in the house in her own office and on a computer, she seldom left the house and never without Chris. They went out every Friday night and that was my opportunity to go into the house, Paddles would fetch me and we would lie on the lounge carpet and chat. Tuna glared at us until she got bored and went to bed and Duke and Tangier were men of habit and they always settled into their basket early in the evening. When we heard the garage door open it was my cue to leave through the window and go to the car to greet Su and Chris.

My weight was a problem and winter was fast approaching. I had lost a lot of my coat and looked more like I had a grey skin covering than a coat. Our coats are supposed to thicken with the approach of winter; my coat was fast falling out. Winter seemed to come early, maybe it was just because I was so thin, so hungry all the time but there it was fast getting really cold.

I no longer slept on the bonnet of the car, I climbed up onto the shelves to the pillows, it was more protected in the corner, and it was warm once I settled in and buried down deep into the pile of pillows.

Rufus seemed to be more hostile than ever to me and that was probably due to the fact that he believed me to have this cosy home and had still not invited him in for a bite.

That was the deal, a deal I made, he made and I accepted by default and out of hunger. Now he probably thought I was just rude and reneged on the deal. I did feel bad about not being totally truthful with him and obviously my sleeping in the garage where he could not see me made him believe I actually was in the house. He saw me out and about with Paddles a lot and probably also thought I had abandoned his friendship. I still was not ready to put my pride in my pocket and come clean with him. I wanted to, I really did but I just could not do it.

Eating Paddles left overs was wonderful but my body needed more, each day Paddles wanted to go out and walk around, jump up and down, but to do this it needed energy and if I just lay in the sun I would not burn up so much energy but living on the little food she left me, was not enough.

Robert encouraged me to eat with him and his friends regularly to supplement my diet and I appreciated his offers and generosity but in truth I was getting ill. I still had not made any in roads into getting any closer to living in the house. The garbage food made me throw up a lot.

The food I ate from Paddles' left overs was tasty, fresh and good clean grub, the food I ate with Robert made me physically sick and I had more belly ache more often so it was all counterproductive as even the good stuff was not staying down. It was also embarrassing to have a condition like this with Rufus always glaring at me, the other strays commenting and asking why "my people" don't take me to the vet. That they had heard from other house cats that they have vets when they are ill. It is all a thing of pride you know so now I had to run behind the houses and deep into the bushes to get sick so no one saw me either. I was becoming very stressed.

"You do realise that you have to get in there soon pal, this weather is not going to hold." Robert said one night.

I was trying, I really was, but the Su human kept chasing me out. She still believed I had a home next door and just liked being at their house. Chris always greeted me, always stroked me. I really liked him.

"Well buddy, you need to do this else you are going to freeze and it is not a nice thing to see."

Chris left every day for work in the morning and returned late afternoon. I would always run up to the car and be right at his feet when he opened the door, I enjoyed the stroking and attention and it always made Rufus look harder at me. He really did resent this. I know his human never stroked him, his hair was long even for a cat it was really long but he was tatty, greasy and did not smell very good either, so his human only fed him and expected him to be in her house at night. She never brushed him or bathed him, not that cats generally bathed but poor Rufus did look a mess. The human contact I had been receiving was not sitting well with him, but I still missed my old friend. My old smelly friend Rufus. I always enjoyed his long drawn out stories and memories.

Winter was upon us. Chris came out the house with a warm jacket on and pointed the remote at the garage and the most amazing thing happened, an answer to my prayers, the garage door broke. It no longer worked on the remote control. The steel arm that swung the doors open from the motor snapped. A mighty crack and then the metal bar clanking on the cement just missing the boot of the car.

Chris was irritated at this, picking up the broken steel arm and placing it in the corner, reaching up to the motor and disabling the automatic setting. A deep long sigh. He manually opened the door and drove the car out. Leaving them standing open for the day.

I am sure the "crook" owner was informed as some workmen did come around and we all stood around looking up at the mechanism but obviously it was not going to be repaired in a hurry, seemed like Robert was right from the start, the crook never repaired anything.

So now the door had to be manually operated. In order to open the door Chris had to push them open and drive the car out and then get out of the car to close them again. When she came home he had to get out of the car, open the gates and after he drove in, he had to close them again.

Robert and I discussed this and he smashed all my hopes to a million shattered pieces.

"Buddy, you have to move fast now, this is no longer a matter to be taken lightly, rumour in the pipes has it on good authority that these people are leaving soon, in fact they only had a six months lease on the property, they are leaving in summer, they are fed up with the crook, the broken garage is the last straw apparently, the stove was broken, they fixed it, all the wiring, cost a fortune, the leak in the bathroom, man, you know that was a big mess around the toilet, so they have spent money and the crook will never pay them back so they are planning not to renew the lease, so buddy unless you want to rewind back to nothing, you need to make a plan and take action."

The thought of being totally abandoned again was too much to bear. I was depressed, I had not even reached any stability and was well on the road to total abandonment again, the thought of the dark closed up house, and the emptiness of it all was enough to give me nightmares. I literally had very little to lose but in my small world, everything. My pride was false as it stood now; I was pretending to have a home with loving people, to have to go back to Rufus as abandoned again, it was just too much for me to think about. I would be in a worse position than before as Rufus would know I lied to him and he would not forgive me so I would have nothing but rats and garbage as a future.

That night I never slept a wink. I lay awake all night staring at the walls, listening to the wind scream through the doors, the gap under the doors threw shadows from the trees blowing in the wind, every noise made my ears turn in different directions, I was a wreck.

The next day when Chris arrived home, he had to stop the car outside of the garage gate, go and open the gate and then drive the car in. He left the car door open while he did this; in fact he left the car engine running. I jumped into the car and sat on the passenger seat. He got back in and saw me, he stroked my head and said, "hello you", you want to go for a little ride hmmm?"

He was obviously nibbling on biltong on the way home, the packet was on the seat. I just thought to myself, "Oh, I could do with some of that" and amazingly he asked, "do you want some biltong?" and offered me a small piece. I gobbled it and he gave me another bigger piece that did not touch sides, so he fed me the rest of the bag. That was seriously good. He got out of the car and asked me if I was coming. I said "naah, i'll hang for a while" and he said, "okay boy, you hang there for a while, I'll come back later and lock up." He left the window open for me. He took his jacket and bag and went into the house.

I bounced out of the car and Robert was halfway scurrying to meet me.

"Dude, that was awesome, You got his attention."

"Robert, wait, did you hear what he said, I think he understood me."

"I know, I saw it."

Dinner time was coming up, I went to sit at the door. The wind had picked up but the kitchen window was open. I jumped up and saw all the house cats being fed. I thought hard in my head, and said out loud, "Please give me some."

Chris looked up at me and said, "well Duke if you are going to play with your food, there is someone else who will eat it for you." Duke just looked at him and walked out of the kitchen. The next thing I knew the door opened, I heard a jingle of keys and a bowl of food was placed on the step for me. "Enjoy." He said and went back into the house. Oh I did, I certainly did. I was not stealing this food, I was given it. I ate slowly and relished each bite. I heard the

Su asking, "why didn't Duke eat" and heard Chris saying, "he is overfed and fussy, he has opinions again, I gave it to the stray."

"Stray?, no he is the neighbours cat"

"No he isn't, I asked them, he is not theirs, he is definitely homeless."

Yes, Yes, okay I was insulted a bit, but at least Chris knew I had no home. I went back to the car and instead of sleeping on the top cushions I climbed back into the front seat and cuddled up.

It was late when Chris came out to lock up the car, he saw me sleeping on the front seat, leaned into the window, stroked my head and said, "sleep tight little one, the car is insured, no harm" and left.

As the door closed shut, I heard Robert say, "It's going to be okay buddy, goodnight." And for no real specific reason I felt tears run down my face.

Chapter 6

The following morning I was up and out of the car early. I sat in the sun and later heard the door open, it was very cold out even though the sun was shining. We were now in the peak of winter. Cris came out, greeted me and opened the garage doors. She started the car and reversed, the car, left it running came back and closed the garage and left for work.

If you could find a spot in the sun where it was protected from wind, it was a pleasant enough day.

Paddles came out and sat in the sun with me. She said, 'We are moving you know". My throat closed at the thought even though Robert had warned me there was trouble brewing with the landlady who was a crook and who was up to her tricks again. "The lady who owns the place is trying to steal money from my people, they signed a six month lease and she has told them that she wants them to stay for a year but Cris wants to move to the coast but now the landlady says she will not return their deposit so there was a big fight, so Cris says she will not tolerate it and we have to move out of this house."

"Paddles, that is terrible news." I did not know what else to say, tell her I was so afraid? Tell her I would not have food again?, tell her I am at the total point of desperation?, I just sat and stared at her with wide eyes.

We spent the day talking in the sun and eventually she said she was too cold and was going to sit with Duke in the house. I waited for Chris. It was dark when he arrived even though it was not too late. He pulled up and opened the car door, he got out and went to open the garage doors, I jumped into the warm car, the heater was on and it was cosy. Chris drove into the garage and got out, closed the doors and came back to the car. "Stay in the car boy, I will bring you some food later."

I stayed in the car peeping over the dash, listening for the door to open. Some time later I heard all the house cats being called for their dinner, I waited, nothing. I smelt human food cooking and then heard Chris washing the dishes. He always washed the dishes. Nothing. I wondered if I had been forgotten. Robert came to the car wheel. "Lot going on still, there is still hope pal."

Some of the lights went off in the house. Now I worried, they were getting ready to go to bed, they slept upstairs. The lounge light and dinning room light went out. I heard the keys in the door. I sat up. Chris came out with two bowls, and a towel under her arm, he looked back to see if anyone was watching. No, Su had gone upstairs. He brought the food to the car, placed the small towel on the front seat floor and places a full bowl of food, meat vegetables and gravy in the one bowl on the towel, and another bowl of milk, not just milk, warmed milk.

"Enjoy little man, I'll see you in the morning".

I ate slowly, making every mouthful last, it was so tasty, the milk was liquid heaven down my throat. No one needed to wash my bowls, I cleaned every trace of food and milk. I lay on the drivers seat, I opened a lazy eye now and then to look with pride at my bowls. My bowls, my supper, my towel, I had stuff now.

Morning came and with it Chris and the computer bag, greetings and smiles. He left for work as he did every morning. My bowls remained in the car.

That evening, when he arrived home, the same ritual ensued of getting the car into the garage, but when I jumped in I saw my bowls were gone from the spot I left them in and my towel was folded onto the seat. He saw me looking at the towel.

"Don't worry boy, I need to wash them and bring them back with some food in them" he said.

"Oh, I was not worried" I kidded. I was very worried.

"See you later, stay warm inside the car now." I settled in for a wait again. I felt good about this. It was freezing and I was warm in the car. I looked at the back seat, there was a blanket spread onto the one side, a warm cuddly blanket. I had seen Chris go to the boot and pull something from it. I was too busy checking on my bowls to notice.

This car arrangement went on for a few nights and now I had this snugly blanket to crawl into each night. I was fed and I was warm. The Friday night arrived and Chris came home earlier, he always did on Fridays. I was sitting in my car waiting for Chris to bring my dinner and while I waited Robert came out. "Pal, you are making inroads now. Good on you. Time is running out, they are leaving here at the month end. That is less than fourteen days away..."

Robert was not even finished what he was saying when the door opened and I heard both Cris and Su's voices. "What should we call him?" Su asked.

"Just get him in and warm and we can decide once he is settled".

Before I knew what was happening the car door opened and I was lifted into the air and when I realised what was happening I was in the house standing in front of my bowls of food. My meat and gravy and my milk. All the house cats were sitting in various places looking at me. Tangier with his dull expression, Duke with his deep frown disapproving of the situation and sweet Paddles came over to me.

"You going to live with us now. Chris got Su to agree that you cannot live outside alone, that you are still a boy, isn't it exciting?, well don't just stand there, eat your food."

I ate shyly with an audience, they soon grew bored with me and went their own ways but I finished every scrap. "Here, have some more ", Su said. "Oh, thank you" I said, and ate that too. I was full, I could not eat another scrap. I eyed the room.

"Hmmm, you can sleep anywhere on that side" Paddles said. I looked over to the side she indicated. It was the lounge, and there was a lovely heater on in it too. There was also a giant fish tank with a light and lots of fish in it. I jumped up there. The light made the top cover warm.

"I think he should be called Sox" he has two white sport socks on his front paws, Cris said.

"I think that is a perfect name for him" "Sox".

Everyone was looking at me. I felt like my heart was going to explode out of my chest. I could not believe it. I had a name now, I had a home, I had bowls and food all my dreams had come true.

"Well Sox, welcome to our home, so you have picked your spot have you." Su said as she put a big fluffy blanket on top of the fish tank for me to sleep on.

More disapproving looks from the others.

Later that night everyone went to bed except Duke. He came over and stood at the bottom of the fish tank looking up at me.

"Young man, there are rules in this house."

And he laid down the law of what I could do and what I could not do. He took it upon himself to show me the ropes and told me where the toilet is. He told me that no one sleeps upstairs with the humans. Some have their sleeping places in the study and in Su's office, some in the lounge. He showed me the windows that were left open at night and told me never to invite strangers home.

Tuna the old irritable cat came over, looked at me, hissed and went to bed. I could not help noticing she hissed at everyone so I did not take it personally.

When morning came the kibble bowls were washed and refilled, breakfast. I had not eaten breakfast in months. Warm milk for afters, oh my word, this was amazing I thought. After breakfast I went out with Paddles. She went to climb in the trees and I quickly went over to the neighbours garage. Robert popped out from behind discarded boxes. "I heard everything "He said, I was hiding in the airbrick.

"Good on you.... SOX? is it? Well pleased to meet you Sox. You are home."

"Robert, thank you, thank you so much for all your help, and your friendship. I do not know what I would have done without you."

"Well it was a pleasure, as much as I could help as a rat. So you will be moving on soon. Hear you are going to a house now. Should meet up with a lot of my cousins hmmm?"

Robert and I spent as much time as we could together in the last days, I had to be careful with paddles being close to me all the time. Once everyone went to bed I would come out through the kitchen window and visit Robert. We spoke of all the things going on in the house, not that I needed to really tell him anything he already did not know with him sneaking in under the pipes and into the air bricks, watching everything with his beady little black eyes but we still discussed it over and over.

Rufus all but ignored me nowadays. He was still angry I had not invited him for a meal and I had tried to tell him why and how difficult it was with Duke and Tangier and Tuna always around, and that Paddles watched and saw everything but he just chose not to understand.

There were more stray cats, more strangers now than before, a lot with babies and food was harder to find now than it was when I was homeless. The bigger male strangers were more aggressive as they were hungrier each night so there was a lot of fighting and howling going on each night. I was so grateful to have a home.

Each night just before lock up time, Cris would call all of us into the house to check we were all safe and each one of us in turn were brushed. It was one of the best parts of the day, the stoking and the brushing, the human contact.

When I watched the brushing and grooming the first night I was amazed. Every night Chris sat on the lounge carpet and one by one we were brushed from head to tail. I was sure Rufus would have enjoyed this very much but his human had so little interest in anything but her TV set. We all had very shiny coats, my coat was very thin due to lack of food over the months. I also was given medicine which tasted like awful to help me with my weak stomach. Chris said my stomach produced too much acid from the bad food I was eating out of the rubbish bins for so long. More and more I was able to keep my food down which was allowing me to put on a little weight.

Once Chris went up to bed, Paddles and I sometimes went out again but at the first sign of any stray strangers we bolted back home to our own safety. We knew that if we were in any fighting Chris would not allow us out at night.

During the long winter days, I know the days are technically shorter but with it being so cold they seemed long, Paddles and I spent our days exploring and visiting the other cats and catching the leaves that fell from the trees.

Robert and I spoke often, he was always scurrying around, new neighbours, new places and things for him to explore, his meetings and the hundreds of cousins he had, always in the bins, all the little beady eyes watching the night, the goings on, the twitching long whiskers, the many long yellow teeth, that was the life of a rat. I once watched how he moved all his new children who all had their eyes closed still as they were so young from one side of the garage to the other and then around the corner into the drain pipe, all little rats holding onto the tail of the one in front of him with his tiny little mouth like a little rat train and Robert like the train master directing the traffic, telling them to be quick and quiet so that they did not attract attention of the cats. Robert was always busy.

Soon enough the day came for us to prepare for our move. Chris and Su had many boxes. How did I not realise this with my original people, that when humans put their things in boxes they were moving away. I made it my mission to sit in each box so that I would not be forgotten behind again.

"Its okay Sox, you are definitely going with us, we wont leave you behind, promise." Su said.

I was just making sure. Each time a car door opened I jumped in, I liked sitting in cars.

The truck came and the household was packed into it. Tuna, Tangier, Tuna and Duke were put into the car. Cris called to me. "Sox, are you coming boyo?" He opened the door. I was in like a flash. I jumped onto the back window of the car, looking through the window I saw Rufus on the pool wall, he nodded his chin at me. I looked up the drive way and Robert was standing on his hind legs, waving, "Go well Pal, Go well Sox." I looked at the pool wall again and Rufus was gone.

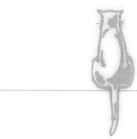

Chapter 7

Oh wow, this was so exciting, the trip was long, it seemed so as I had never been in a car before, I could not remember being in a car before. I mean a moving car. After a while I was not feeling very well with all the other cars going past us so fast. Paddles told me to swallow a lot. She knew about moving cars, she had been in them a few times. I did as she said and before I knew it we stopped and the doors opened.

We arrived at our new home. I bounced out and looked around. Big trees, big garden, we had a swimming pool of our own. No stay cats about. Oh, I spoke too soon. Up above me there was one in the tree. Man, she could make a noise. She was the neighbours cat, a girl and a very noisy one. Paddles and her took an instant dislike to each other. She was small like Paddles, pretty too with a lot more fur. Paddles hissed at her, then growled at her and ran into out home. This was going to be fun.

We settled into a routine soon enough and my favourite place was to lie on the driveway. This was a wide driveway and it had a huge palisade gate in front of it, I could see all the happenings on the other side of the gate without feeling threatened on my side.

Occasionally the neighbours cat and Paddles got into a fight with Paddles determined that we owned the tree and she was just as determined that she would share it with us. I always ran away from the scuffles. I still was not much of a fighter.

I had put on a little weight but in comparison to the other cats I was still very thin, where they walked I swaggered like a cowboys still. I also liked the pool area, Su had grown a border of mustard seed plants around the pool edge and it made bushes which had lovely yellow flowers on them, I liked sniffing the flowers. They attracted bees, so many bees but bees did not worry me and we sniffed them together. I liked playing in and out of the big bushes and yellow flowers.

Life was good. Chris went back to work and our days resumes the routine of before. It was now summer again and the days were warm, the nights so warm we slept outside most of the night on the patio chairs. I loved this house, this home, my home but it was a time of discontent. Chris and Su were fighting a lot over someone called Adam. Adam turned out to be Chris's son. I met Adam once or twice before but did not know they were family, he was a nice human, he liked us all. He always stroked me.

Things were going badly for Adam. I heard Chris say, "if we do not help him he is to be homeless". My heart stopped in my chest. My little voice in its dryness squeaked out…. "Help him, we will take him, don't let him be homeless." I was concerned. I stayed close. I listened in. Much discussion of how to help him. "Yes, I appealed, help him, he can share my bed, he can have half my food." As I looked at Chris, I could see the worry in his eyes. Adam did not have a job, he had had a motorbike accident, he had lost his job as a dancing instructor, he was hurt, he was in trouble, so much to take in.

"Where was he, how is he living, is he in a garage, winter is coming, will he have bowls and towels and blankets, did he have a friend like Robert to help him?" My mind raced.

We had a garden cottage, I heard Su say "we will put a bed in the cottage, use these tables, lets fix the shower." Help was indeed at hand.

Adam arrived with Chris one afternoon, I ran up to the car, "Hello Adam, I am Sox, remember me? I am glad you are not homeless..." and stopped right there, mid sentence.

The biggest bushiest grey and white cat I ever saw in my life stepped out of the car followed by an equally massive smoother ginger and white cat and then Adam. The grey one's name was Mogwai and the ginger was called Smeigel. I shrunk in my thin skin. Smeigle looked at me and dashed around the house. Mogwai flopped down onto the bricks. His paws looked like the hand of a small human. They were giants.

I decided I was better off up the tree. Paddles was up there laughing down at me. "Sox, relax, I know them, they are only boys still. They were babies when they came to us before. I used to look after them. They wont hurt you."

"So you say, have you seen the size of them?"

"Well you are a baby if you are threatened by them. They are well mannered and darlings. I have known them since they were days old. Come let's go say hello."

She bounced out of the tree and rounded the house. Smeigle was clearly very upset, sitting around the side of the house.

"Bad trip? Swallow Smeigle, the bad feeling will pass." She licked his ear. He seemed to calm down.

"I do not like car trips, they make me feel so bad."

"This is Sox, he came to live with us a while ago."

"Howzit Sox, Belch" "Sorry, Have you seen my brother?"

"Mogwai is on the driveway, he seems okay."

"Nothing gets him down. Belch, sorry"

Mogwai came around the house, he had a menacing way of walking, he kicked his front legs with a flick of the foot, my eyes grew wide again, "So what's for supper?" He said...

What I thought were the most intimidating cats turned out to be so kind and sweet.

Mogwai was huge but a real baby boy at heart. He needed a lot of attention, he stayed close to thecottage that Adam moved into, he like to lie in the sun as well. He ate a lot of food. He ate at one meal what three of us ate collectively. Smeigle was more aggressive and he patrolled the perimeter of the property ensuring no strangers came over our wall. He was gentle around us but he did not like strangers at all. He also liked the big tree in the front and also backed Paddles up in chasing the neighbour away.

Summer was hotter than I could remember, or maybe it was because I was putting on some weight, but even Smeigle with his lighter colouring had to have cream put on the tips of his ears to protect him from the sun.

Life was excellent. I could barley remember being homeless. I did occasionally think about Robert and Rufus. Mogwai reminded me a lot of Rufus. He was the same breed but Mogwai was well cared for and brushed until his coat was shiny and clean every day. One thing I had never experienced that was new to me was a bath.

One Sunday Chris ran water into the big tub of the second bathroom and I was playing in my mustard bushes with the bees and looked up and saw a screeching mess of a black ball of fur, wet and hissing. I recognised the voice only now it was a hundred times more angry.

She had had a bath. I had had the misfortune to get wet in the rain and I knew cats did not like water, I did not like being wet. Before I knew what hit me I was summarily lifted into the air and dumped into the bath too. I was mortified, I was wet from nose to tail, and foamed with actually nice smelling stuff. The water was warm, this was a whole new experience for me. I just kept still as a rock. Chris rinsed me and soaped me again, rinsed and into a towel. I was taken outside and dried off and set free into the garden. One by one we were all bathed. Summer baths they called it.

Duke bleated like a sheep, Tangier being deaf made a sound I had never heard and never want to hear again either. Paddles bathed with dignity, she told us to "get over yourselves", it was nice to be clean and get rid of all the winter oils on her coat.

Smeigle objected strongly as well. He was also fur and razor blades.

I learnt over time that each one of these cats had a story to tell. Each one was abandoned in some way. The ginger boys, they were twins, they lived on top of a building in centre city, they were kept in a cage through freezing winter until Su took them in. Tangier went deaf at an early age. Tuna was about to be drowned by her owner as a baby if someone did not take her in. Chris's friend took her in but when she became ill and passed away Chris adopted her. She was 18 yeas old so she was really old for a cat and everyone respected her and she took no nonsense from us. Paddles was a wild cat and lived in a garden with her mom until road workers separated her from her mom and she was found by Chris and rescued as a baby. Smeigle and Mogwai were rescued on the road by Adam as they were placed in a box on a street. So each of us had our own story to tell although Paddles was still a baby and could not really remember life before Chris, Tuna also was a very small baby when she was rescued but she missed her human mom very much still. Tangier never spoke and Duke was always full of stories and opinions. The big boys were only a few weeks old when Adam found them and also did not remember much before they were rescued.

The amazing thing of living with all my new friends was that we all had different personalities and each of us were treated by our humans as individuals. All of us had favourite foods and Chris and Su always made sure that when those foods were around we were sure to get some of it.

We all had our favourite spots to lie in and we gave each other space and respect. Tuna was the boss being the oldest cat.

Our humans were so nice and so caring. If any one of us fell ill we were immediately taken to the vet. Our food was in abundance and heaters were available when the weather was cold. Even in summer, if the days turned cold the heaters would go on for us. Chris would feel our ears and a small fact few humans know is that cats get very cold. Cats do not like storms, Chris understood this, and Paddles was terrified on storms as was Smeigle, so it was quiet normal for us to see cupboard doors standing open if a storm was coming as Chris and Su knew that we would feel safer inside the cupboards while the storms raged.

Summer came and went and winter was brutal. We spent most of our time indoors.

We overheard Chris and Su speaking about leaving. Certain words still made me nervous. This peaked my interest. Leaving? Abandonment? What was happening.

Soon it became apparent that we were leaving. They were planning. Apparently a life long dream to live at the coast. Duke listened in to conversations Su had on the phone. He reported back. Quotes. She was getting relocation quotes to move us. All seven of us. To move us 600 kilometers. Flights for humans. Trucks for furniture. Strange people came and made notes of the furniture. Boxes were delivered. Adam was packing. Chris was packing. Su was packing. Su did most of the packing. Winter had passed and we were into summer and it was time to go. Apparently Chris and Su had waited out winter so that the seven of us could travel in the warmth of summer and not feel the ill effects of winter travel.

The house was abuzz with packing and telephone calls.

Something serious was going on. This seemed to have a greater intensity than the last move, what made it so different I wondered.

We were moving across the country. We were going to the coast and we were not all going to be moving together. We as cats were going alone. The humans would not be with us. I was nervous. What if they forget one of us. What if one of us gets lost. I needed that reassuring voice in the car telling em we are nearly home, that it is going to be alright, to relax, I did not like this one bit.

I began to lose weight again. My nerves were bad. I could not show the others. I had to keep this to myself. Oh how I wish Robert were around to talk to.

I tried to talk to Paddles. She just told me to relax. Humans move around a lot. I asked her where the coast was. She said she did not know. She said it was probably down the road. I did not think so, this had a different feel to it.

I spoke to the neighbour cat. She said she came from the coast and she flew in an aeroplane. She said the noise was deafening, she said she was very sick from the aeroplane and it was very far away. She said she would rather run away than do it again. I did not know what an aeroplane was, she pointed to the sky when a grey spot flew up over us, so far away, not like a bird, I tried to watch it for a long time, I felt sick. I could not go into a grey spot in the sky I decided. Maybe I should also run away, but to who, and to where. Homeless again? Live on the streets? It was not an option.

I was very confused. I stayed on my drive way, I had gotten so used to the barking across the road I did not notice it before now, but now it worked on my last already freyed nerve. I marched over to his gate.

"What is it with you and all the barking, who are you barking at?"

He looked at me and said, "And what is it to you, go lie at your gate on your nice hot bricks and leave me alone."

"My word but you are rude and I am tired of listening to you barking, I am trying to have a nervous breakdown and you are interrupting me." I yelled at him, brave for the first time in my life out of sheer nervousness of the situation I was in.

"Seriously? Why, what's wrong, can I help you?"

I made friends with the dog across the road. His name was Bruno. He was okay, he was an old Labrador. He was on the other side of the fence. I was safe on my side. I now understood how Robert felt when he first met me. I knew he was lonely as he barked at nothing and everything.

"The coast you say", he said. He seemed like an authority on it.

"Yes, we are going to the coast, how far is it and what is it?" I asked.

"I grew up at the coast when I was a pup, Oh I remember it so well, like it was yesterday my boy, sandy beaches, dog smells, urinating on rocks, wet feet, running with my human in water, wonderful place it is." He smiled.

Seriously? I thought, sand was good for the cat box, dog smells I generally avoided, urinating on rocks not for me, running in water, was he talking about rain?

He seemed to go into a dream like state remembering his pup days. He sat down on the grass and told me long stories of his life as a pup with his human and then one day they just stopped going to the beach, his human gave him to these older humans who took him on a long car trip and he has never seen the beach again or his original human. He lived here now but they did not take him for walks, they did not really do much with him other than feed him and bath him occasionally and yell at him barking at everything and at nothing.

He protected the house, barked at the postman and the paper delivery man, lay on the patio and slept, he said he was lonely and wished he had a friend to talk to. He said if I was going to the coast I was a very lucky cat.

I told him about the aeroplane and he just laughed at me. He said I should just relax, the neighbour cat was a drama queen, she made up awful stories most of the time.

I felt better about things and went to tell the others. Tuna seemed to take the most interest in my report. She sent me back to ask more questions. She definitely seemed less hissy now. When I came back and told her that my dog friend said it is warmer at the coast she definitely seemed more relaxed about where we were going.

Tuna was getting old and she was also feeling the cold, she was thin, her teeth gave her trouble so it made her moody a lot but she was an alright old lady to me. She had really foul breath though.

She never left the house but asked me one night to take her over to speak to Bruno. We waited until the road was very quiet and the humans had gone to bed and I took her over the road and introduced her to Bruno.

She asked him questions and eventually I was too tired to sit and listen to these two oldies and left and went to bed on my patio chair. When I woke up Tuna was in the house so she managed to come home alright.

Chapter 8

The house was now almost totally packed up. Boxes replaced space in the lounge and dinning room.

Chris was not going to work. He was helping with the final packing and seemingly doing a lot of work on that laptop computer.

Paddles said it was payments. She always knew it was payments as she saw the blue screen and then heard the beeps on the cell phone.

There was talk of the aeroplane but not for us. It was for the humans. I worried about them being in the grey blip in the sky. It was so small, how were they to fit in it and how did they get so high into the air and where did it go that it crossed the sky so fast. I watched for every grey blip.

Then the morning came, a hot blistering day, it was different, something was very different about it. My humans were on edge, I could feel it. Then the noise. A loud thunderous noise came down the road. It stopped at our gates. The gates opened and a grinding noise came up the drive and a thunderous crash landed at the front door. I peeped out of the window. My first reaction was to run and hide in the garden but the doors and windows were all closed now.

Chris and Adam came to each of us one by one. Adam held us firmly in his large hands, Chris opened our mouths and shot some medicine into our throats. "Oh Yuk". It was so bitter.

He stroked our heads, said "now you will be calm for your trip. You will be fine. We will see you tonight."

One by one we were taken out of the house and put into the cage at the front door. It was one very large cage with divisions in it. I was alone in my section. Paddles and Tuna were put into a section together. Duke and tangier in a section together and Mogwai and Smeigle together. Su had put cardboard at the bottom of each section and also blankets for us to lie on. The medicine had made us drowsy and I was feeling very calm. Tangiers eye lids were half closed already. Paddles was asleep next to Tuna.

Some men lifted the cage on either side and we were hitched to a tailer and canvas rolls flapped down and covered us totally. A car started and we were moving. It was just fine. I was already dreaming. My last vision was men moving furniture and boxes out of the house and in to the truck just as the canvass roll flapped down.

I woke up and this was not right, this was very wrong. We were sitting in our cage as we were put in hours ago, but now the cage was not on the trailer, it was on the grass. There was a tree above us and it was raining, fine soft rain. The top of the cage had a cover so the rain passed to the sides. I looked around, We were all together. Tuna was awake and sitting watching something in the distance. Paddles was waking up. Tangier and Duke were awake. Smeigle and Mogwai were still asleep.

"Where are we" Paddles asked.

"We are at a farm of sorts, I saw some animals and chickens" Tuna said.

"What are we doing at a farm, is this the coast?" I asked

"No, this is not the coast. Our furniture is over there" she indicated with her head.

We all looked around. The furniture was standing on another piece of grass, close to a house. I could not understand why our furniture would be outside a house. I was so confused. Where were our people.

"Shssss, pretend you are sleeping" Tuna hissed at us.

We all lay down and acted asleep again. The short fat man who came to our house weeks ago came to the cage, he looked in. The woman came with him, the one who was all smiles the day she took money from Chris at our home. The woman brought food and opened the cages just enough to squeeze the bowls in. She slammed them shut again. None of us moved.

"They will eat when they wake up" she said to the man.

His phone rang. "Hello, Yes, we are running a bit late, we had to wait for the big truck to arrive and they are nearly finished packing it and then we will be on the road."

It was Chris. No more pretending to be asleep. We all knew that voice and we loved that voice. Oh how I loved that voice. But it was angry now. I still loved the voice even angry. We sat up.

"What do you mean you will be on your way, where are my cats."

"No they are here, they are fine."

"where is "here"? He bellowed into the phone.

"No well you see we had to offload the trucks at the smallholding and then reload to the pantechnicon truck so they are here with me."

"It is eight o clock, you were expected to be here with our cats and our furniture at six oc clock and you are telling em you have not even left yet, have my cats eaten, what about water?"

"Ag No, we have fed them and they have water", he lied.

"Jan, what time will you be here with my animals and furniture?"

"No we are leaving now, they are just finishing the loading and then we are leaving so we will be there first thing in the morning."

"Where are my cats sleeping tonight?"

"We will put them in a room with paper so they can mess if they want"

"paper? These are cats not dogs, they need sand"

"okay, jaa, we can give them sand"

"Jan, I expect you to be here at seven sharp in the morning and there had better be nothing wrong with any of those animals"

"No No, don't worry Chris, they are all fine."

Click

"There is no way we can get there by seven, ag, put the water bowls in and cover these cats up and lets go, they are just cats."

The cages were opened slightly again and water bowls were put in and slammed shut and the roll of canvass came down again. We were in the black of the night but it was at least warm. I needed to use the toilet only we did not have one. I would have to hold in till morning.

I lay listening to every sound in the night, I could hear the twitching of Tuna's ears. She did not go back to sleep. She was awake and alert.

The light was creeping in from the bottom of the canvass covers.

"Heads up, someone is coming" Tuna said.

It was the woman. She came and changed our water and rolled back the canvass.

"Hello, oh you are pretty" she said to Mogwai.

"I am not pretty, I am a boy" he said back

"Don't speak to them" Tuna hissed at him.

She walked away, we waited. So much for being at the coast first thing. We were still in the same place and we were still looking at our furniture on the grass now covered with canvass as well. The plants were standing a little away from the furniture. Oh we all knew Su was going to be upset, they were dropped and the sand had spilled out of some and others were lying on their side clearly broken.

Su loved her plants and her garden so much, and these were so carefully packed and now they were broken and lying out of their soil.

There was noise, cars were coming. A small truck was coming. It stopped in front of the house. It smelled of car oil and smelt hot. It had a blue light on the top of it. Two men got out of the car and one from the back of the truck. He had a hurt face. His mouth was swollen and cut, he had blood on his shirt.

The men went to the house and banged on the door. Jan opened the door, there was shouting between him and the man with the hurt face. The other men grabbed Jan and tied his hands behind his back. They all left in the van. The woman went behind them in another car. She was talking on her phone as she left. This looked very bad for us.

"It is going to be okay." Tuna said. "We need to be calm and wait, someone will come".

Strangely we all believed her. Her calmness made us calm. We settled in and waited, what else could we do.

The sun was getting hot again but we were under the tree which had big branches and many leaves, we would be okay here for a while but we were all hungry now. The last decent meal we had was breakfast the day before.

I fell asleep, I had extra space in my section as I was on my own, I could stretch out.

I awoke to a strange voice

"Hello down there"

"Hello" Tuna said

"Hi, I am up here"

"We can't see you up there, come down from up there."

There was a shuffle and then we saw him.

A skinny house cat. He had so many colours he looked like he ran through a paint box and he had one brown eye and one green eye.

"Hi, I am Tom" he said

"Well hello Tom" Tuna said. "Are these people your people?"

"Yes, Lynn is".

So now we knew the woman had a name

"And where may she have run off to" Tuna asked

"Oh she will be back just now, there is always trouble here, we only came to live here a little while ago, but Jan, well he is trouble, he is always hitting the men who work for him."

Tom stopped talking

"And…" Tuna said

"Oh and then the police come and take him away for a while and then she goes and then they both come back."

"And…" Tuna said

Oh my word, this Tom had attention issues, it must be all the colours on him.

"Oh it is only when he drinks too much, only every other day, so you are all on your way somewhere?"

"Well we certainly do not live in this cage young man, so how long would you say they are normally away on these little excursions?"

"Excursions what?"

"How long are they normally away on these little trips with the police people?" she hissed at him

"Oh, not long."

As he spoke we saw the dust rising in the distance, a car coming at speed towards the house again. True to Toms words, Jan and Lynn drove up. She was crying and he was shouting. He also now looked like he had a split in his lip. They were fighting but we could not hear what they were saying.

"Oh, it is always over money"

"Do you always start your sentences with Oh?" Tuna asked

"Oh, what, Oh no, not really" he said, see you. "Good luck"

Chapter 9

We sat under the tree and we saw Jan come out and walk on the patio. Watching him it was clear that he was a man with problems. He was on his cell phone constantly. He walked towards us. His phone rang and he answered.

"Where in the world are you and where are my cats"?

Tears came to my eyes. Our beloved Chris's voice

"We are close, we just had a mechanical problem with the truck, so we had to stop and wait for a part to come" he lied

Tuna sat bold upright and hissed at him. "How can you lie like that, we have not moved from here."

Her hissing got the young boys twitchy and they too hissed at him.

"And my cats are where exactly."

"No they are fine, they are right here."

"Jan, have you fed my cats, do they have water and how are they going to the toilet?"

"No they all went to the toilet before we left and they are fine, yes they have everything they need. Every few hours I stop and open the truck and they get fresh air and I promise they are all fine" he said as he looked at us and lied to Chris.

"How long is it before you reach here" Chris asked

"Ag, No, as soon as the part comes we will put it in, it is a easy job and then we will be there, chop chop now."

Reality was that we were not even close as there and here sounded very far from each other and he was lying all the time.

When the call ended Jan made a call himself.

"You had better get that tuck here fast now, that doctor is calling me all the time and it is going to take us four hours to still load and another 12 hours to get to delivery, so I have told him that we are on the way and we will be there tonight so now you better move it. How long before the truck gets here?"

"Six hours, I cant travel in the night with cats in a truck, yes, yes, jut get it here at least we can load it today."

So that was it. We were going to be here for a long time still.

Lynn came out of the house. "What's happening with the truck"

"Six hours"

"Jan, that doctor is going to go mad, we were supposed to be there last night already."

"I know but what do you want me to do, carry the furniture on my head?"

"I told you not to lend that guy our big truck, I told you he isn't trustworthy"

"well he paid me a lot of money to move his load, the doctor can wait"

"The doctor paid us too."

"Ja well they will have to wait, there is nothing I can do"

"We need to feed these cats"

"Feed them, I am not stopping you" He walked away.

Lynn went out in the car again and came back with food for us, she gave us more water as all the bowls were dry.

"Try not to eat too much or drink too much." Tuna said, we will have to use the toilet and we don't have one.

"I am too hungry to worry about that" Mogwai said as he licked the last of the food from his lips.

"I am not eating this food, it smells funny" Paddles said

"Neither am I" said Duke looking into Tangiers empty bowl. He pushed his over to his brother with a paw.

Neither Tuna nor Paddles ate their food. I ate all of mine and I did not worry about the smell of it. I had known dustbin food.

We fell asleep again, it was hot and here was nothing to do at all.

A long while later we heard an engine, a big engine. The biggest truck in the world came to a stop in front of the house. It was nearly dark again. A car followed the truck. The truck driver jumped out of the truck and Jan came out of the house.

"Where in the world were you guys, do you know how much trouble you have made for me?"

"Ai sorry man, we had a lot of booze to offload in three towns and we had to avoid the cops man, but hey, here are your keys" the man with the filthy jeans said to Jan as he threw the keys into the air at him.

"'Where are the guys to load? I can't load this truck on my own"

"Oh, no we dropped them on the road, you are on your own, sorry, bye now." He said and got into the car and it sped off.

Lynn came out of the house and looked at Jan and burst into tears. "I can't run a business like this."

He followed her into the house and the door closed, the clouds had come over again and it was drizzling. We still had the cover on the top of the cage but the drizzle was blowing into the one side of the cage. There was not much space for Smeigle and Mogwai to move around and both were getting wet on their backs now. Fortunately their coats were very thick.

We saw Tom sitting up at his house licking his paws and for the rest there was no movement around the house. Su's plants were at least getting some water after baking in the sun all day.

"Tuna, what is to become of us?" Paddles whispered in the dark

"We will be okay little one... we will be okay"

"I am scared."

"Lie closer to me, there there, sleep now" I heard Tuna whisper back

No one noticed that Tunas breath was so bad now. She was our strength and he said we were going to be okay and we believed her and in what she said. She was the oldest, she knew everything.

The daylight broke grey and gloomy, it was still raining softly. We were still in the cages and we were all quiet damp with the wind blowing in different directions through the night blowing the rain into the cage. None of us cried out during the night. Tuna calmed us. She spent most of the night talking to us and telling us stories of her past life with her human mom who was no more.

She distracted us with stories of horse racing and walks on the golf course they lived on. She had many stories to tell us of the rats on the golf course and she even made Paddles giggle at herself with memories of running away from the eagles in fear of being lifted up on the golf course. Paddles shared stories of all the friends she made on the golf course. We listened and laughed through the night and before we knew it it was day light again.

I only realised that night what a close relationship Paddles had with Tuna and that Tuna was actually a very sweet old person.

Chapter 10

The house was quiet and there was no movement. We watched the door and the windows, it was light but gloomy weather. Then a light went on. We sat up and stretched out as much as we could in the cages. Another light and then another. The lights on the patio went off.

The door opened and Jan came out, he had a cup in his hand, he drank the steamy liquid and went back into the house. A while later he came back out and got into the car and left.

We were all hungry and thirsty. The water was empty in all the cages. We waited.

The clouds were blowing away and their were patches of blue in the sky again. The rain had stopped.

Jan came back with three men in the car. Immediately they were out of the car he began yelling at them. They all went over to our furniture and they lifted the canvass sheet off it. They folded it and began packing our furniture into the enormous truck that kept us company for the night.

It seemed to take forever for them to lift and move the furniture up the ramp and there was a lot of banging and scuffling coming from inside the truck. It must have been huge inside there if I considered the amount of furniture that we had in our home.

Slowly it went until there was far less furniture on the damp grass than before and soon enough they were lifting the half broken plants into the truck.

Lynn came out to check on us.

"Oh you poor things, you are such a mess in there." She said looking at Mogwai and Smeigle. They had had to use the toilet in the night as they could no longer hold in. Mogwai was angry and Smeigle was embarrassed about it. Lynn went into the house and fetched some tissue paper and opened their cage. She cleaned it out and put fresh paper into it but the blankets were soiled and it smelled bad. We had been in the cage for what seemed like a hundred hours.

We had heard Jan's phone ring many times and we did not even have to listen carefully to hear Chris's voice booming loudly down the phone at him. He continued to lie and continued with his stories until he switched off the phone totally. There had not been any more ringing since the lights went out in the house last night.

Lynn brought out food pouches for us and opened them, reached into each cage and poured the contents into our dishes. She poured fresh water into our water bowls. We ate hungrily and drank the water. Tuna ate all her food as did a now very hungry little Paddles. 'That's a good girl Paddles, keep your strength up."

"Are we going to be okay Tuna? Really okay?" she asked

"We will be fine" Tuna replied and settled in to watch Jan and the men again.

We had grown bored watching them and fell asleep again with full bellies. A mighty roar awoke us.

Jan had started the engine of the truck. We sat up in alarm a little disorientated. Some of the furniture was still on the grass. The men were still going up and down the ramp taking stuff in and in some cases stuff out only to take it back in again.

The plants were all moved into the truck but still furniture was going in. The trucks powerful engine remained running and Tom appeared on the branches of our tree again.

"Looks like you a lot are leaving" he said

"But the truck has started the engine and we are not in it yet" Paddles said to him in an alarmed voice.

"Oh No, that truck has to run for a good while before it can go, warming up." Tom said

"Oh, You lot go in last, you don't want to be near it now with all that smoke all over the place."

Paddles smiled sweetly at him and Tuna hissed at him. He ran off.

The spot where the furniture was standing was now just an very large empty space and the three men were walking towards us. They lifted our cage and walked us over to the truck. With a mighty bang we were in the truck. What was the remains of our water bowls was now all over the blankets and truck floor. We were spun around to face the doors and then they closed.

Pitch black darkness and terrible engine noise. No one said a word. It was like sitting in a black nothing. The air seemed to stop, we seemed to stop breathing altogether.

Then the noise of the engine increased, and then a change of the noise. We began moving. Oh this was so scary, I felt sicker than

I ever had in my life. I heard Paddles whisper to Tuna, "Are we still going to be okay?" and her whisper back, "We will be fine."

The truck stopped but the engine did not. Another clunk and then we were moving again, in the opposite direction. Oh my word, bumps, we were going over bumps in this large truck stuck in this cage. We were sliding from one side to the other. I was still so thin, I banged my ankle on the side of the cage and my chin when we went the other way, I swear I could feel my whiskers were bent.

Then the truck stopped again, the engine sounded different and then we were moving again, smoother, quieter.

"Well we are on our way" Tuna said, "I think the worst of it is over."

"I don't want to be in here" Smeigle said

"None of us do my boy, so lets just settle in." Duke said

Our eyes had adjusted to the pitch blackness of the truck now, we could see each other. It was comforting to have each other. I would have been terrified if I was alone.

We listened to the changing of the engine, the change of the gears of the truck, we could not make out any outside sounds. The same sounds over and over and then they changed. We seemed to be going a lot faster and the engine was a lot quieter. We heard music. We heard Jan singing with the music. He could not sing well. He sounded bad, he sounded very bad indeed.

The phone rang. Oh I was so happy to hear that ring. Then I heard Chris's voice, it sounded different, more hollow.

"It is coming from this side of us" Mogwai said. "it is a hands free kit, Adam has one" he said.

We heard, "Where are you and where are my cats?"

'You see the thing is this, that we could not get the part we needed, when they brought it back it was the wrong size so it had to go back to the nearest town and then they were closed so we had to wait until this morning and change the part and the truck is now fixed and we are on the way now"

"Jan, we left on Tuesday morning, you were supposed to have been here Tuesday night, we slept on the floor in a totally empty house on Tuesday night, on Wednesday you told me you were on your way, we slept on the floor again, yesterday you told me you were not far away from me and we were on the floor again and today is Friday, I am not interested in your lies any longer, I have arranged another truck to meet you and take my furniture and cats off your truck and bring them to me. Tell me where you are and we will come to you, I do not care if I have to come all the way back."

"No really, I tell you what, give me half and hour and I will stop and I will take a picture of the cats and send it to you, I am nearly by you."

Click.... silence!

"He is spitting mad now." Tuna said

She had not even completed the sentence when the phone rang again

"Jan, this is Susan, I want to know where you are right now."

"No Susan, like I told Chris, we are on the way now. We had a bit of trouble, but now it is all good."

"What time will you be here Jan, exactly what time?"

"No like I told Chris, as soon as we get close, I will call you so you can lead me in."

Click...

The phone rang again

"Jan,..."

Immediately Mogwai and Smeigle both sat up.

"Jan, this is Adam, please we are very worried about the cats, please tell us how far away you are from us."

"No Adam, like I told Susan, the cats are fine. I will send you a picture of them soon when I stop for Diesel and then you can see for yourself."

The engines roared and we seemed to be going faster than ever before.

We waited in silence and then we slowed, and more and turned and slowed and then stopped but the engines did not stop and then they did. Nothing but the blackness.

A banging noise on the door right next to us and then the light. Oh my word, the light was like a million daggers in our eyes. Jan flung the doors open and the fresh air filled the space. Slowly we adjusted our eyes to the extreme light flowing into the truck.

For the first time we noticed that the cover was off the top of the cage. The doors were open and Jan disappeared. We stood up and stretched as best as we could in the confined spaces. Mogwai climbed over Smeigle and Tuna hissed at him to behave himself. There was no way he could get out of the cage so it was best to sit still.

Jan reappeared with a big bottle of water and poured it in a fashion into our water bowls, missing more than he got it into the bowls.

Then a flash of brighter light with his phone. He had taken a photo of us.

"Clearly he wants them to see we have water." Tuna said.

He fiddled with his phone and waited. It rang almost immediately.

"Thank you for the picture Jan, I see the cats are fine but how far away are you. It is after lunch again and we are still waiting."

"No, Chris, we are nearly there, like I told you, if it wasn't for the part it would have been fine."

"Jan, just get here, please."

Click

Jan disappeared again, leaving the truck open, we watched cars flying past us on the road at high speed. We were at a garage. We heard Jan talking on his phone again. He was telling Lynn he just stopped to get more fuel and food. He told her that he had sent Chris a picture of us.

"Ag nee wat, they believe anything I say, what can they do, I will get there when I get there"

The truck roared to life again and he was back at the door. Slam went the heavy doors and we were back in the blackness. Slowly the truck changed from backward to forwards, we slid to this side and that, and then we settled in again, the speed increased and we were back on the road again. The music started up again, the terrible singing.

One by one we fell asleep after a long drink of water, a flood of fresh air and darkness, what else was there to do.

Chapter 11

I slept deeply, I dreamt, I woke and I stretched out, fortunate to have my space to myself I listened to Mogwai and Smeigle for a while.

"Take your foot out of my face."

"Well mind your tail out of my mouth"

I listened to Duke talking to Paddles. "There is no point in trying to tell him anything, he does not hear me, I just push him but he keeps lying on my tail."

"Well don't be so rough with him, he cant understand what is going on, it is not like he can be told or listen in on the phone calls. Just be kind to him."

"Stop it all of you, stop bickering." Tuna said

"You will all behave, if we allow chaos to over take our minds we will all begin fighting and it will make things so much worse. This man has clearly lied to our people all the way along, he is a dishonourable person and we can be glad that he did not just open these cages and leave us all behind in a bush somewhere. At least we are safe and we are going to see our people again. If we fight we may aggravate an already volatile situation" She stated.

Okay, I had been with humans for some time but some of these words I did not understand.

"Psst Paddles, what did she say?"

"She said behave else Jan may open the doors and put us all out, like out in the middle of nowhere"

"And we will be homeless I asked?" She nodded, "Oh Okay" I whispered back

Homeless, my greatest fear.

I curled myself into a tight ball and kept as still as I could. I would not contribute to anything that could possibly make me homeless again.

I just listened to the sounds of the truck.

The phone rang again.

"Where are you now?" Chris demanded

"Ag like I said, we are going but the traffic is very heavy and I have to go slow up the hills, I can't go fast like a normal car."

Jan was going really fast, we could tell

"So at least tell me what town you are in Jan."

"Hello, you are breaking up, I can't really hear you"

Jan was lying again, we could hear Chris clearly, he just did not want to answer the question.

The engine roared and the speed must have been really fast as for the first time we heard car hooters and then the very loud honk of Jan's horn hooter. It sounded like a blast.

I fell asleep again. During the trip we had learned the difference of being close to other cars and busy streets like when we reached a town and went through a town to when Jan was going to stop or go straight through the town. He slowed down going through towns and sometimes we stopped and then he went through nine gears to get us going again. When we were awake it became a game to count the gears he was using and if he would stop or not. Most of the time he slowed and then accelerated. Paddles said this was to prevent stopping the truck totally at traffic lights.

The trip seemed like it was never going to end. We did not know what time of day it was other than by our hunger or thirst. It seemed to be supper time. Jan was going fast all the time and we had no more water left. We had all resigned ourselves to using our blankets now as our toilet boxes. We just scrunched them into the corners of the spaces we had. We were past holding in.

The gears changed, the truck was turning, we were stopping, the brakes squealed. The truck stopped. The door banged, footsteps, our doors clanged, opened and no bright light poured in. it was dark. It was night. There was luminous light from the petrol station, the same colours like the one opposite our road where I was homeless before. Green lights.

Jan looked into our cages. He grunted and walked away. He went into the store. He returned with food. he passed us and went to his drivers door. He slammed that shut again and disappeared again. He reappeared with the water bottle, he sploshed water through the top of the cages again into our water bowls and on us.

He pointed his phone at us again, flash of bright light and we were blinded again. He fiddles with his phone and almost immediately it rang.

"I am beyond fighting with you Jan, I just want my cats and my furniture. Where are you now."

"You see the thing is I had problems with the trailer lights so I had to pull off and have it sorted because if I get stopped they will not allow me to go further so I had to have the problem fixed in one of the towns."

We all went wide eyed at how easily Jan could come up with such lies. We had not stopped. We had not fixed any lights. We had been motoring at speed for hours. We had even heard him telling Lynn that he was not going to stop at all the weigh bridges and take his chances to make up time.

"So how come you did not tell me this earlier Jan?"

"Ag you know I just want to get to you as soon as possible, I did not want to worry you with more problems."

"Well thanks for the picture of the cats I see they are okay but they also need to eat."

"There is not place I can buy them food here, I am out in the bush there is nothing around me for miles and I can't leave the truck to go into a shop and it is late now." He lied again, we were standing right beside a store and I could see our food on the shelf at the doorway.

"Yes, Jan I do understand that, I have their food, I bought them food today so that when they get here I can feed them immediately"

"Okay, well we are close, I will call you as soon as we get to your area."

Jan kept saying we, but it was only him in the truck. Unless he was refereeing to us as part of his we.

Jan climbed back into the cab, he left his door open, he had a very large mirror on the side of the door, we could see everything he was doing in the cab.

He ate his dinner, drank his coffee and went to sleep. The wind had picked up and it was getting quiet cold in the truck given we were now wet with his generosity of water splashes.

A while later he woke up and went back into the store with his flask at the coffee counter. He came out and started the engine. The truck roared, he reversed it to a pump and cut the engine again. It was a while before he came around the truck and slammed the doors on us again. Blackness. The engine roared, the gears changed, we slid to and fro again, we settled and the speed picked up.

"I hate that he does that, I am too old to be thrown around like this." Tuna complained into the darkness.

The phone rang

"Jan, this is Chris, look, stop playing around, exactly where are you, it is dark and late again it seems like we get to sleep on the floor and my poor cats live in the truck, what is going on exactly?"

"Chris, I promise, I will be there tonight still, just wait for me, I am not far from you now."

Click

"Best we try to sleep now." Tuna stated

No one said a word.

I did not sleep immediately, I lay awake wondering about if we would ever be "home" again. I was not technically homeless now, we were together and I was happy I had a family, we were seven cats in this cage, all feeling different things, Paddles was frightened and she hated noise. Duke was irritable as his joints were giving him trouble and he could not stand up and had not been able to for the last three days and night. Tangier was deaf so the noise did not bother him as he could not hear it at all so he was just himself, quiet. The twins were irritated at being locked up and they were large and needed space. I was panic filled all the time and I hated the noise. Tuna was our strength and we looked at her for guidance and we did as she told us to.

I fell asleep deciding I was a lot better off in this truck with my friends than I was way back then living in the garage next to the oil spill.

Chapter 12

I slept until the truck lurched and stopped. I awoke, confused as to where I was, my mind had drifted into peaceful sleep, in my dream I was happy. The pitch blackness of the truck I awoke to was scary at first until my eyes adjusted and I saw the others. Also sitting upright and dead quiet.

We heard the door of the cab open and slam, then the clunking of the doors right next to our cage. A flood of fresh air filled the truck and we were looking into the bight neon lights of another petrol station.

Jan was making a call on his phone.

"Hello, Hello, Chris, I am here by you, so can you lead me in?"

"How are my cats Jan" Chris demanded to know

"They are fine, I am looking at them right now, they are all calm, will take another picture and send it to you."

"If you are that close, leave the pictures and tell me where you are"

"I am at the garage by your area but need you to lead me in now"

"Okay from there it is easy, come back out the garage, at the stop street cross over, first road turn left, then immediately right and then next left and you are in our road, we are no 15, the house third from the end of the road on the left side." Chris explained.

"okay so it is over the road, first left then right then left, no 15, third from the end on left side?"

"Yes, that is correct."

"Okay, I will be there in a few minutes"

The phone clicked off.

We all looked at each other in amazement. This time Jan was not lying. This seemed real and it seemed like Chris and Susan were right near us. Jan shouted to a man who was sitting against the wall.

"Hey you, do you want to earn some money, I want someone to carry furniture for me."

The man jumped up and came towards Jan. "Do you have a friend that can help as well?"

"No boss, I am alone."

"Oh well, you will have to work hard then. Get into the truck."

The doors slammed shut on us again and the truck began moving as soon as Jan closed his door.

Now cats do not know terribly much about things but we do know directions. Some of my kind have been able to travel vast distances back to their original homes.

So when the truck stopped we all began to calculate the directions, over the road and so we went over the road. The truck slowed down and Chris had said turn left, and we turned left really slowly. This had to be a place where there were houses and small streets and that must be the reason we were travelling so slowly.

We were excited, I could hear my heart beating in my ears, we were home, nearly.

The truck travelled on and then slowed down and almost stopped and we turned right.

We were all tense, this was it, we were nearly home, such a long journey, we had been in these cages for what seemed like forever and now we were going to be home.

The tuck travelled on slowly and then slowed again. Oh my word, we were turning left, the last turn, we were on the home stretch. How many houses were in this road I wondered. The tuck travelled slowly, we seemed to be going around a bend and slightly up a hill, and then we slowed and stopped.

Nothing. We waited in the darkness barely breathing at all. The truck gears grinded and we were going backwards. Slowly and then stopped. The door opened and Jan jumped out of the truck shouting at the man.

"Maak oop, open up the side doors."

The flood of fresh air again, the blackness of the night but then we all saw them almost at the same time.

The driveway to the house was uphill and steep and walking towards us was Susan and Adam, half walking half running and behind them was Chris.

"I told you I would get us here if you all behaved." Tuna said

"Oh, I am so happy to see them." Paddles said

"They are not going to be happy to see me like this." Mogwai said looking at his thick coat

"Oh get over yourself Pretty boy." Smeigle said as he tried to climb over his brother again

"All of you be quiet" Duke said, "I just want to get out of here now and I am going to tell them everything"

Duke was the tattletale of us all, he reported everything we did to Susan but he did not realise it was not Su that understood him, it was Chris.

Tangier just sat in his deaf bewilderment and smiled at us all. He knew his people and he was also happy to have reached home after being in the truck for so long.

We looked at our humans and they at us, happy to see each other and amazed that we had all come so far and we were reunited again.

"Get them out of this truck immediately Jan, this is a disgrace that they have had to be cooped up like this for this time, this is not what we paid you for."

Adam and the strange man jumped up into the truck and began shifting our cage, carefully they lowered us down and we were on solid ground again. They lifted a side each and carried us up the drive way and into the open garage where they set the cage down.

Chris had began preparing our supper in bowls, we could see him scooping the food out of the pouches and into the bowls on the shelf of the garage in front of us. The smell of the rich food and gravy drove me bonkers. I began dribbling.

He opened each cage one by one and put our food in front of us. I jumped straight in. oh, the wonderful taste of it after so many days in that cage, no supper, no breakfast, I do not even remember when we ate last but I was enjoying each mouthful.

"I am not hungry right now" Paddles said "I just need to find my feet again."

I tried to reach through the cage between us with my long skinny arm to take some of her food but it was too far away.

"Seriously Sox, are you going to eat everything at a time like this?" she asked me

"Well yes, I am starving and a growing boy." I replied

"Help yourself." She snubbed me

Everyone else ate and then one by one we were taken out of the cages and up stairs and up more stairs to a massive bedroom and bathroom. One by one each of us was washed off with bubbly hot cloths and dried with towels. We were dirty, we had been wet with Jan's method of giving us water, we had been dust blown while sitting in the truck with the doors open and we had used the toilet in our own cages and blankets. We smelt awful but because we were all in the same boat we did not realise it or see it on each other until we arrived home.

Mogwai was the worst of us as his coat is so thick and long and he objected all through his grooming process.

We were allowed to sit upstairs in this strange place and room while our human's brought in some of the furniture. We heard Su complain and fight with Jan about the fact it was close to midnight and he had brought only one helper.

Again we heard Jan tell lies about the fact that it was the only guy who could come with him to the coast. We knew he had just collected the man on the other corner at the garage. The humans brought as much as they could into the house at that hour but decided to wait until daylight to bring in the rest.

We slept on the floor that night which was not bad at all as it was a carpet and the house was warm.

The next morning we were allowed to wonder around the house. It was a massive three story house with a garden and a pool of its own and so many places to explore.

The humans brought in all the furniture and it was wonderful to rub against it again. I still did not understand what the big deal was about the coast and why we had to travel so far to get here until Paddles took me onto the top patio and we looked out at the horizon.

"That, Sox, is the coast, the end of the line of the land, the big blue out there is the ocean which is just water and water and more water"

"Oh my Paddles, it is so nice to look at."

"Well that is why we have come so far, this is where Chris and Su wanted to live for the longest time, so now we are all home at last."

Home, such a lovely word. I looked at my humans from the top of my world, the third floor balcony and at my cat family sitting in various places they chose in the sun and realised that I was home, not because of the journey we had travelled, not because of the time it took, but because of the people I was with, because I belonged, because my heart was here, with my family, the people I loved, worried about and needed to be with, home is where my heart is. Home is here.

I am Sox and I am home.